Bear Claws

Pam Scheunemann

Illustrated by Neena Chawla

Consulting Editor, Diane Craig, M.A./Reading Specialist

ABDO
Publishing Company

Published by ABDO Publishing Company, 4940 Viking Drive, Edina, Minnesota 55435.

Printed in the United States.

Credits
Edited by: Pam Price
Curriculum Coordinator: Nancy Tuminelly
Cover and Interior Design and Production: Mighty Media
Photo Credits: Jerry Bargar/CritterZone.com, Bill Noerenberg, Dennis Olivero/Northern Light Nature Photography, John Pennoyer/Impressions of Nature, Photodisc

Library of Congress Cataloging-in-Publication Data

Scheunemann, Pam, 1955-
   Bear claws / Pam Scheunemann ; illustrated by Neena Chawla.
      p. cm. -- (Fact & fiction. Animal tales)
   Summary: Harry has a wonderful time playing and eating special treats with his cousin Teddy at their family reunion, but soon it is time to go back home to his mother's den at the Woodland Inn. Includes facts about black bears.
   ISBN 1-59679-925-0 (hardcover)
   ISBN 1-59679-926-9 (paperback)
   [1. Family reunions--Fiction. 2. Cousins--Fiction. 3. Black bear--Fiction. 4. Bears--Fiction.]
I. Chawla, Neena, ill. II. Title. III. Series.

   PZ7.S34424Bea 2006
   [E]--dc22
                                                                      2005027825

SandCastle Level: Fluent

SandCastle™ books are created by a professional team of educators, reading specialists, and content developers around five essential components—phonemic awareness, phonics, vocabulary, text comprehension, and fluency—to assist young readers as they develop reading skills and strategies and increase their general knowledge. All books are written, reviewed, and levels for guided reading, early reading intervention, and Accelerated Reader® programs for use in shared, guided, and independent reading and writing activities to support a balanced approach to literacy instruction. The SandCastle™ series has four levels that correspond to early literacy development. The levels help teachers and parents select appropriate books for young readers.

Emerging Readers	Beginning Readers	Transitional Readers	Fluent Readers
(no flags)	(1 flag)	(2 flags)	(3 flags)

These levels are meant only as a guide. All levels are subject to change.

FACT & FiCTioN

This series provides early fluent readers the opportunity to develop reading comprehension strategies and increase fluency. These books are appropriate for guided, shared, and independent reading.

FACT The left-hand pages incorporate realistic photographs to enhance readers' understanding of informational text.

FiCTioN The right-hand pages engage readers with an entertaining, narrative story that is supported by whimsical illustrations.

The Fact and Fiction pages can be read separately to improve comprehension through questioning, predicting, making inferences, and summarizing. They can also be read side-by-side, in spreads, which encourages students to explore and examine different writing styles.

FACT OR **FiCTioN?** This fun quiz helps reinforce students' understanding of what is real and not real.

SPEED READ The text-only version of each section includes word-count rulers for fluency practice and assessment.

GLOSSARY Higher-level vocabulary and concepts are defined in the glossary.

SandCastle™ would like to hear from you.

Tell us your stories about reading this book. What was your favorite page? Was there something hard that you needed help with? Share the ups and downs of learning to read. To get posted on the ABDO Publishing Company Web site, send us an e-mail at:

sandcastle@abdopublishing.com

American black bears live in forests as far south as Florida and as far north as Canada.

Harry peeks out of his mother's den at the Woodland Inn.

"Let's get scampering, Harry! We're going to the family reunion at Bear Springs!" Mama Bear says.

5

Most black bears are black or dark brown.
They can also be lighter shades of brown.

Once they're on their way, Mama says, "We're meeting your grandma and cousins from down south. If you behave, you'll get some of Grandma's famous bear claws!"

7

Black bears are omnivores and eat both plants and meat. Berries, fruits, nuts, acorns, plants, and insects make up the main part of a bear's diet.

At the reunion, Harry meets his cousin Teddy. They lick their lips when they see all of the good food, especially Grandma's famous bear claws!

9

Black bears' short, curved claws help them climb trees. Despite their size, bears can climb a tree quickly.

Harry and Teddy become fast friends.
Their favorite pastime is climbing trees.
They also enjoy playing baseball with
the other cubs.

Black bears have a good homing instinct and can find their way back after being moved 40 to 50 miles away.

When the days get cooler, Mama says, "We need to get going. It's almost time to hibernate!"

Harry cries, "But cousin Teddy doesn't have to hibernate yet!"

"Your cousins have a shorter journey to get home," Mama says, "so they don't have to leave yet."

September

13

The length of time a bear hibernates depends on food availability and the length of winter. In the north, they may hibernate for seven months or more.

When it's time to leave, Grandma gives
them a basket of bear claws for the trip.
On the way home, Harry talks of nothing
but Teddy and the fun they had together.

15

Bears' dens might be in hollow trees, caves, burrows, or holes dug in the ground. They line their dens with leaves, grass, and twigs.

When they reach the Woodland Inn,
Mama picks out a warm comforter
for Harry before they go into their
den and get settled.

Woodland
Inn

vacancy

17

Black bears are very smart. Their long-term memory is exceptional.

Harry snuggles under his comforter and writes a letter to Teddy. As the snow starts to fall, he drifts off to a long winter's sleep and dreams of baseball and Grandma's bear claws.

FACT OR Fiction?

Read each statement below. Then decide whether it's from the FACT section or the Fiction section!

1. Not all black bears are black.

2. The amount of food bears can find affects how long they hibernate.

3. Bears play baseball.

4. Bears sleep under comforters.

American black bears live in forests as far south as   10
Florida and as far north as Canada.   17

Most black bears are black or dark brown. They can   27
also be lighter shades of brown.   33

Black bears are omnivores and eat both plants and   42
meat. Berries, fruits, nuts, acorns, plants, and insects   50
make up the main part of a bear's diet.   59

Black bears' short, curved claws help them climb   67
trees. Despite their size, bears can climb a tree quickly.   77

Black bears have a good homing instinct and can find   87
their way back after being moved 40 to 50 miles away.   98

The length of time a bear hibernates depends on   107
food availability and the length of winter. In the north,   117
they may hibernate for seven months or more.   125

Bears' dens might be in hollow trees, caves,   133
burrows, or holes dug in the ground. They line their   143
dens with leaves, grass, and twigs.   149

Black bears are very smart. Their long-term memory   158
is exceptional.   160

Harry peeks out of his mother's den at the   9
Woodland Inn.   11

"Let's get scampering, Harry! We're going to   18
the family reunion at Bear Springs!" Mama Bear   26
says.   27

Once they're on their way, Mama says, "We're   35
meeting your grandma and cousins from down   42
south. If you behave, you'll get some of   50
Grandma's famous bear claws!"   54

At the reunion, Harry meets his cousin Teddy.   62
They lick their lips when they see all of the good   73
food, especially Grandma's famous bear claws!   79

Harry and Teddy become fast friends. Their   86
favorite pastime is climbing trees. They also   93
enjoy playing baseball with the other cubs.   100

When the days get cooler, Mama says, "We   108
need to get going. It's almost time to hibernate!"   117

Harry cries, "But cousin Teddy doesn't have to   125
hibernate yet!"   127

"Your cousins have a shorter journey to get home," Mama says, "so they don't have to leave yet."

When it's time to leave, Grandma gives them a basket of bear claws for the trip. On the way home, Harry talks of nothing but Teddy and the fun they had together.

When they reach the Woodland Inn, Mama picks out a warm comforter for Harry before they go into their den and get settled.

Harry snuggles under his comforter and writes a letter to Teddy. As the snow starts to fall, he drifts off to a long winter's sleep and dreams of baseball and Grandma's bear claws.

GLOSSARY

burrow. a hole or tunnel dug in the ground by an animal for use as shelter

exceptional. better than most others

hibernate. to pass the winter in a deep sleep

intelligent. having the ability to acquire and use information

omnivore. one who eats both meat and plants

pastime. an enjoyable activity done in one's spare time

reunion. a gathering of a group that has not been together for a long time

To see a complete list of SandCastle™ books and other nonfiction titles from ABDO Publishing Company, visit www.abdopublishing.com or contact us at:
4940 Viking Drive, Edina, Minnesota 55435 • 1-800-800-1312 • fax: 1-952-831-1632